Cookie
the
Seder Cat

Story and Photographs
by
Nechama Liss-Levinson

Oreo Cookie Press

ISBN
978-0615467757

Oreo Cookie Press

For our dear Seder guests
family and friends
Then and Now

Have you met our sweet
cat named Cookie? Cookie
is five years old.

Cookie loves to celebrate the holidays with us. She is very happy when she knows that Passover is coming soon.

"Meow, meow, meow," she says.

Cookie likes to help us
clean the house for
Passover.

When it's
time to search for
the bread crumbs
or chametz,
Cookie is always the
first one ready.

Ready, set, go!

Cookie looks for crumbs
that could be hiding in
our bed.

Peek a boo, Cookie!
 Where are you?

Peek a boo, Cookie!
 We see you!

The day before Passover is Cookie's favorite day.

Cookie helps us to polish the shiny holiday candlesticks with her whiskers.

Swish, swish, swish.

Cookie is so excited when we bring the boxes of special Passover dishes up from the basement. After we take all the dishes out of their boxes,
we
find
Cookie
hiding
in every
box.

Cookie helps us to
make the charoset,
the mixture of apples
and nuts and wine
that we will eat at
the Seder.

"Meow, meow, meow"
    she says as we go
        chop chop chop.

Cookie is ready to
make her favorite
food for the Seder
dinner, the potato
kugel.

Uh oh! Oh no!
Silly Cookie.

You can't eat the kugel
until we bake it in
the oven!

No, no, no.

Cookie always invites her sister Oreo to come over to her house for the Seder.

They love to celebrate Passover together.

"Welcome to our Seder, dear sister, Oreo."

"Thanks for inviting me, Cookie. Happy Passover!"

Cookie loves to make Kiddush.
She says the blessing
"*Borei Pri Hagafen*"
for
all
four
cups
of
grape
juice.

Oreo says "Amen" and
then she drinks up her
whole cup.

Amen. Amen. Amen. Amen.

Oreo knows how to say
the blessing

"*Ha Motzei Lechem
Min HaAretz*"

before eating the matzah.

But Cookie can't wait to eat
    the crunchy matzah!

        Crunch, crunch, crunch.

Now the Seder is almost over. It's time to steal the piece of matzah called the Afikomen and hide it.

Uh oh! Oh no! Silly Cookie!

Instead of stealing the Afikomen,
Cookie steals the
bone from
the Seder plate.

"Yum, yum, yum," she purrs.

Luckily Oreo remembered
Cookie's game of
"Steal the Bone"
from last year and she
brought another bone for
the Seder plate.

Good thinking!

Thanks a lot Oreo.

Todah rabah.
Todah rabah.
Todah rabah.

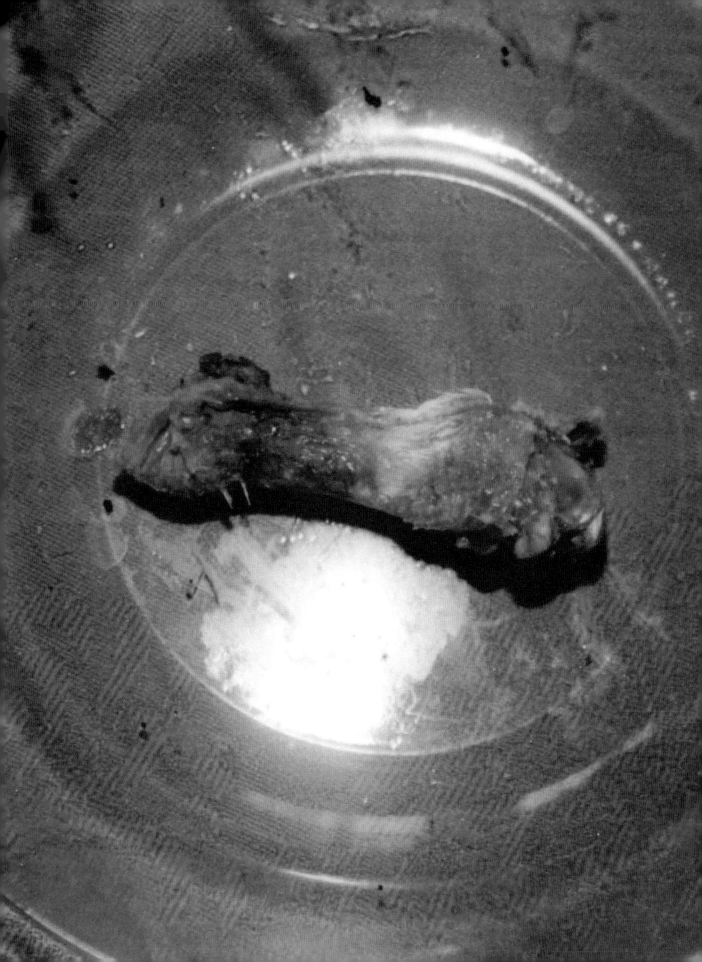

Just in time,
Oreo found
the Afikomen.

She hopes to get a
special treat for
finding it.

What a nice present
Cookie gives to her
sister Oreo for finding
the missing matzah.

At the end of the Seder
we all sing about

the dog
and the cat
and the goat
that my dad bought....

Oh look!
Cookie has fallen asleep.

Shh, shh, shh.

In her dreams,
Cookie the Seder Cat
is singing
the Four Questions
at next year's Seder.

Ma Nishtana?
    Ma Nishtana?
        Ma Nishtana?

וַאֲפִילוּ כֻּלָנוּ חֲכָמִים

Va'afilu koolnu chachomim: And even if we are people who see ourselves as "smart"— as persons who already know the facts and the details, even then we are still obliged to tell the story of the departure from Mitzrayim.

כֻּלָנוּ נְבוֹנִים

Koolnu nevonoch: And if we are people who see ourselves as "wise," as people who already have spiritual knowingness and understanding, even then, we are still obliged to tell the story of the departure from Mitzrayim.

See you at next year's Seder!

Made in the USA
Charleston, SC
03 April 2011